Brady Brady
and the Puck on the Pond

Written by *Mary Shaw*
Illustrated by *Chuck Temple*

PUBLISHED BY
BRADY BRADY INC.

Hey Kids! Never go near a pond without adult supervision, like a coach or parent. The ice may be too thin to skate on and could be extremely dangerous.

Published in Canada in 2005 by

Brady Brady Inc.
P.O. Box 367
Waterloo, Ontario
Canada
N2J 4A4

Library and Archives Canada Cataloguing in Publication

Shaw, Mary, 1965 -
Brady Brady and the Puck on the Pond / written by Mary Shaw; illustrated by Chuck Temple
Contributing Writer: Alison Lafrance
For children aged 4-8

ISBN 1-897169-07-8

I. Temple, Chuck, 1962- II. Title.

PS8587.H3473B7323   2005   jC813'.6   C2005-905533-2

Just when Brady thought he had all of the makings for a fun game of shinny on his great rink, his friends are
invited to play on an even greater rink! Friendships are tested – will the Icehogs stay together?

Printed and bound in Canada

Keep adding to your Brady Brady book collection. Other titles include:

- **Brady Brady and the Great Rink**
- **Brady Brady and the Runaway Goalie**
- **Brady Brady and the Twirlin' Torpedo**
- **Brady Brady and the Singing Tree**
- **Brady Brady and the Super Skater**
- **Brady Brady and the Big Mistake**
- **Brady Brady and the Great Exchange**
- **Brady Brady and the Most Important Game**
- **Brady Brady and the MVP**
- **Brady Brady and the Puck on the Pond**

Brady loved winter. He loved winter because he loved
to skate. Brady would skate on his backyard rink
every chance he got.

One afternoon, Brady and a few of his friends were playing a
game of shinny when Freddie, one of Brady's teammates on the
Icehogs, came rushing into the backyard.

"Brady Brady! You should see the *size* of the hockey rink on my grandpa's pond!" said Freddie excitedly. "It's the biggest and best rink *ever!* You guys should come over and play!"

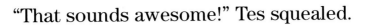

"That sounds awesome!" Tes squealed.

"I can't wait!" Kev added.

"Let's go put the puck on the pond!" Chester hollered.

Brady watched his friends as they rushed off the ice to follow Freddie. This was the first time that his friends wanted to play shinny somewhere else. Brady gripped his hockey stick tightly, and tried not to show how sad he felt.

"You guys go ahead and have fun. I have to stay and help my dad with some chores," Brady lied. "Maybe I'll catch up with you later."

As the kids gathered at the pond, Freddie's grandpa high-fived them, and showed them the cool benches he had made out of snow. Freddie was quick to point out the blue lines and red circle in the middle of the ice.

"See?" said Freddie,
"Just like Brady
Brady's rink!"

The Icehogs were having way too much fun on Freddie's rink to miss Brady. They thought it was cool to play on such a big rink. When they took turns sitting on the bench, Freddie's grandpa brought them cups of hot chocolate filled with colored marshmallows.

"This is the *best* rink ever!" said Tes
between sips of hot chocolate.

The next morning, Brady wolfed down his breakfast, grabbed his stick, and headed out to his backyard rink. He wanted to have his rink all shoveled off and ready for the Icehogs – but Brady's friends had something else in mind.

"Hey, Brady Brady," said Tree, "we're going over to Freddie's pond. Do you want us to wait while you get your skates?"

"No, you go ahead. I have to help my dad again," said Brady with a frown. "I'll catch up with you guys later." But Brady knew he wouldn't be catching up with them later.

He put on his skates and practiced his slapshot with his dog, Hatrick. It wasn't as much fun as it usually was. Even Hatrick got bored and walked off the ice with the puck between his teeth.

That night at dinner, Brady didn't have much of an appetite.

"What's wrong, Brady Brady?" asked his mother.

"Yeah, you don't seem like yourself lately," said his father. "You've been moping around the house for the last couple of days."

Brady took a deep breath and let out a big sigh. "All of my friends want to play with Freddie instead of me," he explained. "His grandpa has a big ice rink on his pond, with benches made out of snow. The kids don't want to play on my rink anymore. I **won't** play on Freddie's pond – even if it means that I have to stop playing with my friends!"

"You could do that Brady Brady, but don't you think you would be lonely?" his mother asked.

"There's only room for one rink in this neighborhood!" muttered Brady.

The next day, Brady's friends were waiting at the end of his driveway once again. This time Brady convinced them that they should have a game of shinny on **his** rink.

"It's too far to carry all of our equipment to the pond. Anyways… I hear that Freddie doesn't even have any nets," said Brady. "Who's heard of using boots for goalie nets?"

The Icehogs didn't care; they just wanted somewhere to play.

As Freddie shoveled the pond, he wondered
why the Icehogs had not arrived. He thought
everyone was going to meet at the pond first thing in
the morning. After all, his friends seemed to like
playing hockey on his grandpa's pond.

Freddie finished cleaning off the rink, but there was still
no sign of his teammates. He decided to try and
find out what his friends were doing.

As he walked through the neighborhood, he could hear laughter coming from Brady's backyard.

"Hey," said Freddie. "I was waiting for everyone to come and play a game on the pond. What happened?"

"Everyone decided to play on my rink instead," Brady boasted. "Plus, you don't have any hockey nets, so how do you expect us to have a **real** game?"

Freddie turned and left Brady's backyard with his head hung low.

"That wasn't a very nice thing to say to Freddie," whispered Chester. "He's your friend."

Suddenly, Brady didn't feel like playing anymore. He remembered how sad he felt when he had no one to play with. Determined to make things right, Brady knew that he needed to come up with a plan.

"**Wait**!" cried Brady. "I have a great idea! Why don't we meet early tomorrow morning, and we'll surprise Freddie by cleaning off his grandpa's pond! I'm sure he could use a few friends to help him out!" The kids all nodded in agreement.

"I have a couple of old hockey nets that would be perfect for the pond. We can bring them in the morning," said Brady.

Brady got up early the next morning. He grabbed his skates, stick, and his dad's big shovel. His friends were already waiting on his driveway. They gathered up the extra hockey nets and whisked them off to the pond.

"We've got some work to do," said Brady, as he heaved snow over to the side of the frozen pond. Everyone pitched in to help. They even made snowmen to be the "fans in the stands."

When Freddie arrived at the pond, he could not believe his eyes. The ice had been completely shoveled and the old winter boots had been replaced by Brady's hockey nets.

"Hey!" yelled Brady, as Freddie walked over to the benches. "How about a game of shinny?"

As Freddie's face lit up, Brady realized that it was his friends...*not* the rink...that made the game fun!